W9-BSK-889

THERE'S
THIS
THING

PHILOMEL BOOKS
Published by the Penguin Group | Penguin Group (USA) LLC
375 Hudson Street, New York, NY 10014

USA | Canada | UK | Ireland | Australia | New Zealand | India | South Africa | China
penguin.com
A Penguin Random House Company

Copyright © 2014 by Connah Brecon.
Penguin supports copyright. Copyright fuels creativity, encourages diverse voices,
promotes free speech, and creates a vibrant culture. Thank you for buying an authorized
edition of this book and for complying with copyright laws by not reproducing, scanning, or
distributing any part of it in any form without permission. You are supporting writers and
allowing Penguin to continue to publish books for every reader.

Library of Congress Cataloging-in-Publication Data is available upon request.
[Insert CIP]
Manufactured in China
ISBN 978-0-399-16185-8
1 3 5 7 9 10 8 6 4 2

Edited by Michael Green | Design by Semadar Megged | Text set in Loveletter
The art was done digitally.

THERE'S THIS THING

Connah Brecon

Philomel Books
An Imprint of Penguin Group (USA)

For Jackie & Poppy,
my Things.

There's this thing I really like.
I would like to like it
even more.

It's all . . .

and ...

I would like to know it better
but I'm not very brave . . .
And I don't know how to ask.

So I send an **invitation**.

But the postman doesn't know
where it lives.

So I leave a trail of crumbs for it to follow.

I leave a trail of crumbs

I set a trap.

And wait.

And wait.

rrrrrrrrrrrrrr!

But I catch
the **wrong thing!**

I thought I might get it
with an arrow . . .

I miss.

So I try being someone else.

But can't decide who.
I am only myself.

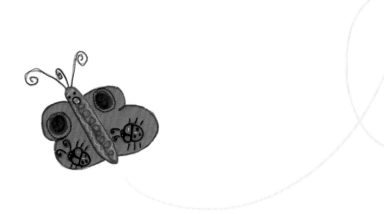

I clear my throat
and try saying all the things in my
head.

re you od at
Will you ste my friend
you
alking?

I've got fish.

I love icecream

I've been on a plane.

I've got red hair.

Squid have beaks and birds too

My Dog has flees

I LOVE

I like Singing

Tadpoles are neat

Hello.

I've got two legs

Why doesn't it notice me?

I really want to share my heart
but I just can't find the
right way to open it.

I think it must not like me.

May I?